The Pumpkin Patch

For my mother, another McNamara

First Aladdin Paperbacks edition September 2003

Text copyright © 2003 by Simon & Schuster
Illustrations copyright © 2003 by Mike Gordon

ALADDIN PAPERBACKS
An imprint of Simon & Schuster Children's Publishing Division
1230 Avenue of the Americas
New York, New York 10020

READY-TO-READ is a registered trademark of Simon & Schuster.
The text of this book was set in Century Schoolbook.
Book design by Sammy Yuen Jr.

Printed in the United States of America
2 4 6 8 10 9 7 5 3 1

Library of Congress Cataloging-in-Publication Data
McNamara, Margaret.
The pumpkin patch / Margaret McNamara ; illustrated by Mike Gordon.—
1st Aladdin Paperbacks ed.
p. cm. — (Robin Hill School) "Ready-to-read."
Summary: Katie finds what she thinks is the perfect pumpkin on a class field trip to a
pumpkin patch, but after her classmates tease her about how small it is, it is up to
Katie's father to show her how perfect her pumpkin can be.
ISBN 0-689-85874-4 (pbk.) — ISBN 0-689-85875-2 (library edition)
[1. Pumpkins—Fiction. 2. Field trips—Fiction.] I. Gordon, Mike, ill. II. Title. III. Series:
McNamara, Margaret. Robin Hill School.
PZ7.M232518Pu 2003 [E]—dc21 2002155809

The Pumpkin Patch

Robin Hill School

Written by Margaret McNamara
Illustrated by Mike Gordon

Ready-to-Read
Aladdin Paperbacks
New York   London   Toronto   Sydney   Singapore

"Put on your coats!"
said Mrs. Connor.

Mrs. Connor's class
was going
on a field trip
to the pumpkin patch!

Katie was ready first.
She could not wait
to find
the perfect pumpkin.

The bus ride was long.

The whole time,
Katie imagined
the perfect pumpkin.

At the pumpkin patch
there were lots and lots
of pumpkins.

PUMPKINS

"You may each
take home
one pumpkin,"
said Mrs. Connor.
"Choose carefully."

Katie began
her search.

She looked
under vines.

She looked in
the straw.

She looked
in the mud.

At last Katie found it—
the perfect pumpkin!

Mrs. Connor's class
got back on the bus.

They showed off
their pumpkins.

"Mine is round,"
said Emma.

"Mine is tall,"
said Ayanna.

"Mine is big," said Neil.

"Look at Katie's pumpkin!"
said James.
"It is so small."

Katie's pumpkin was small.
It was very, very small.

Katie felt bad.
Her pumpkin
was not perfect.

Katie took her pumpkin home.

"I picked a bad pumpkin,"
she told her dad.

"That is not a bad pumpkin,"
he said.
"It is a good pumpkin.
Let me show you."

Katie's dad
cooked the pumpkin.
Then he cut it
into pieces.

Katie mashed the pieces.

And they made a pie.

Katie took the pie
to school.

"My pumpkin was small,"
she said.

"But it was sweet!
Now it is a pie."

The children loved
Katie's pumpkin pie.
"Your pumpkin was perfect!"
said James.